This book
belongs to:

D1625574

BuzzPop

an imprint of Little Bee Books

New York, NY

Copyright © 2019 by Smart Study Co., Ltd. All Rights Reserved.
Pinkfong® Baby Shark™ are licensed trademarks of Smart Study Co., Ltd.

All rights reserved, including the right of reproduction in whole or in part in any form.

BuzzPop and associated colophon are trademarks of Little Bee Books.

For more information about special discounts on bulk purchases, please contact
Little Bee Books at sales@littlebeebooks.com.

Manufactured in China TPL 0421

First Edition

7 9 10 8 6

ISBN 978-1-4998-1072-1

buzzpopbooks.com

pinkfong
BABY SHARK

Ultimate Sticker and Activity Book

Check your answers on pages 63-64.

BuzzPop

Meet the Family!

Baby Shark

Baby Shark lives in the ocean and is curious about everything around him. He likes to sing. When he's scared, he sings to help himself feel brave.

Mommy Shark

There are no limits to the things that Mommy Shark can do! She always listens to Baby Shark and they share a very special bond.

Daddy Shark

Daddy Shark is a strong and mighty hunter. He is much more than just Baby Shark's father, though; the two of them play together like best friends!

Grandma Shark

Grandma Shark likes to read. She is a kind and thoughtful grandma who always has time to spend with Baby Shark.

Grandpa Shark

Grandpa Shark is wise and smart. He is famous for his hot clam buns and he loves to share his love of cooking with Baby Shark.

There are so many sea creatures for Baby Shark to play with!

Mommy Shark is looking for Baby Shark. It's time for lunch!

Yum! The Shark family is eating lunch together.

The Shark Family Orchestra!

Oh, no! The Shark family has lost their instruments. Can you find them and stick them in?

"oh, no!"

Play It Again!

Baby Shark is supposed to be playing the marimba! Can you find the right sticker? Now you can sing along!

doo doo doo doo doo doo doo!

Shark family song,
doo doo doo doo doo!

Join along,
doo doo doo doo doo doo!

Plink!

Plink!

doo doo doo doo doo doo doo!

Color Me Happy!

Grab your colored pencils and color in Baby Shark and all his friends.

Octopus Ice Cream!

Spot the difference: Which ice creams have changed color? Circle them!

Baby Shark is playing hide-and-seek with his friends. Can you spot him?

Shark Art!

Use the handy grid guides to help you copy the different characters.

Baby Shark doo doo doo doo doo doo!

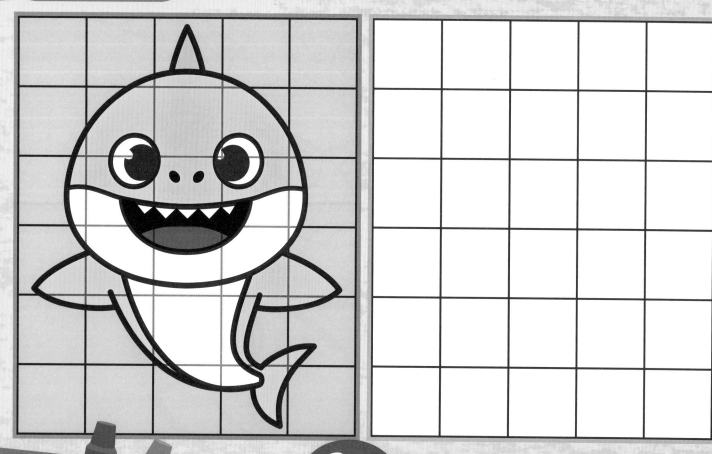

Daddy Shark

doo doo doo doo doo doo!

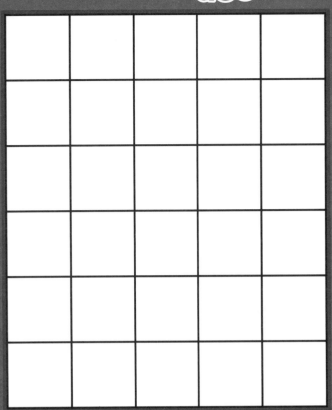

Mommy Shark

doo doo doo doo doo doo!

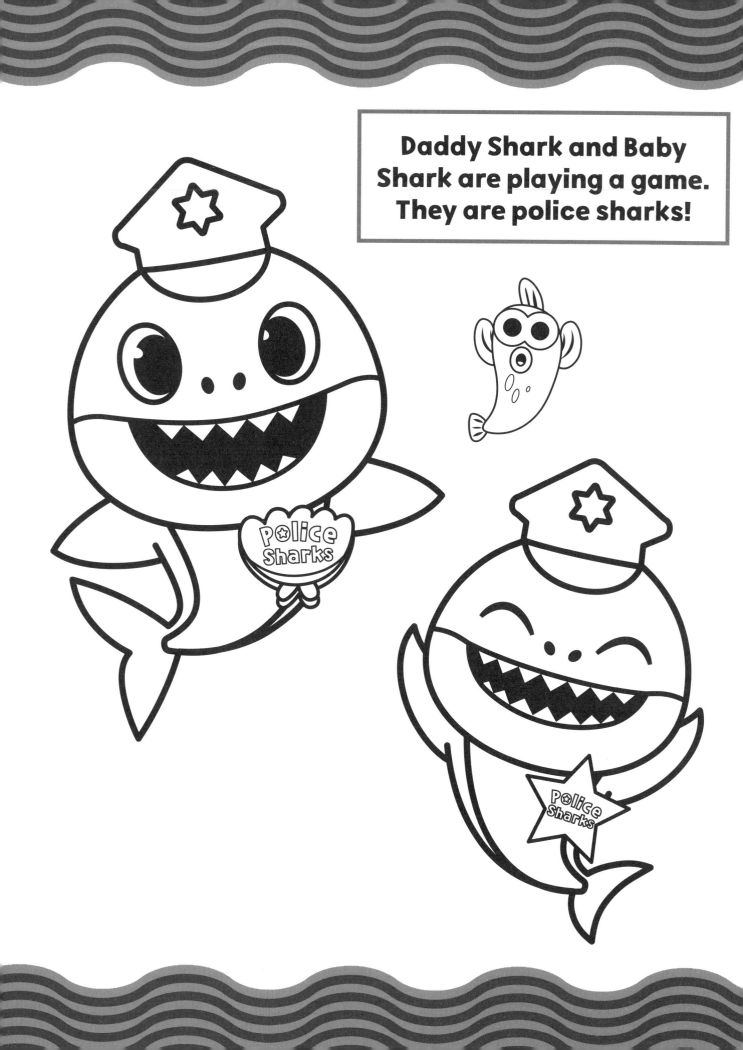

Daddy Shark and Baby Shark are playing a game. They are police sharks!

The police sharks rescue Hammerhead Shark.

Find all the Sea Creatures!

Baby Shark loves to play with all his friends, as long as they don't run away!

Check the box when you find each sea creature.

19

Baby Shark is all over this page!

Sea the Same!

Can you add five stickers to make picture two match picture one?

Color the Rainbow!

Baby Shark and Grandma Shark are having lots of fun! But this picture has lost its color! Use your colored pencils to add the color back. The handy number guide will help you.

23

Sort It Out!

Who should come next? Can you find the right sticker and put it in the right place?

1

2

3

Ask a grown-up to help you cut out Baby Shark, Mommy Shark, and Daddy Shark. You can attach them with some ribbon as shown in the picture.

doo doo doo doo doo doo!

Please ask an adult to help you cut out this page!

Grandpa Shark is happy to see you!

Party time,
doo doo doo doo doo doo!

Police Sharks!

Nee Naw! Baby Police Shark and Daddy Police Shark are here to save the day! If you have a problem, they can solve it.

Weeeeee! Oooooo!

You've earned your Shark Police badge. Stick a star here.

Oh, no! Daddy Shark's and Baby Shark's police hats have gone missing. Can you help them? Find the correct stickers on the sticker pages!

Baby Shark Rescue!

Baby Shark is lost!
Who will find him?
Draw them here.

Baby Shark can play the marimba. Plink! Plink!

Grandma Shark can play the trumpet. Pah-pa-rah!

Treasure Hunt!

Baby Shark is racing his friends. First one to the treasure chest wins!

Winner!

Follow the lines to find out who wins. Everyone gets a balloon from the sticker page!

36

Grandma Shark and Baby Shark have made a sandcastle.

Where's Baby Shark?

Everyone is looking for Baby Shark. Can you find him?

	1	2	3	4	5	6
A	START: →					
B						
C						
D						
E						
F						

ollow these directions
from the start:

Baby Shark is
in square

_____.

7   8   9   10   11   12

39

Grandpa Shark and Baby Shark have made some cakes. Yummy!

Baby Shark gives cakes to all his friends.

Lost Property!

Everyone has lost something! Draw a line to help them find what they're looking for.

Baby Shark has lost his ball....

Mommy Shark has lost her sun hat....

Daddy Shark has lost his police hat....

Grandma Shark has lost her magic wand....

Grandpa Shark has lost his sunglasses....

Grandma Shark is happy to see you!

Baby Shark's Photos!

"Oh, no!"

This is Baby Shark's special photo album! But oh, no! The photos have lost their color. Can you add the correct sticker to each picture?

The Shark family loves a picnic!

Grandpa Shark is going to play some tunes!

Baby Shark and friends are swimming, swimming, swimming!

Baby Shark Is Everywhere!

Baby Shark is being silly and is all over the place! How many times can you spot him?

Baby Shark is in the picture ___ times!

Baby Shark loves to dress up, and today, he's an artist!

Baby Shark is dressed up again, this time as an astronaut!

Doo doo doo doo doo doo!
We love to sing and play.

doo doo doo doo doo doo doo!

Fix the Picture!

Find the missing puzzle piece stickers to complete the picture.

Baby Shark Shadows!

Can you tell who is who by their shadows? Draw a line to match each shark to their shadow.

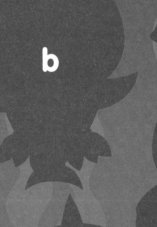

a

b

c

1

d

e

2

3

4

5

Dotty Baby Shark!

Connect the dots to see who is in the picture. Then, color them in!

Baby Shark's Magic Crayons!

Baby Shark can use his magic crayons to color everything. Can you color each picture with the correct color crayon?

RED

GREEN

BLUE

YELLOW

Baby Shark's Friends!

Baby Shark is alone and wants some friends to play with. Can you draw him some?

There are some ideas of who to draw around the page.

Mommy Shark, Daddy Shark, and Baby Shark are playing soccer!

Baby Shark Maze!

Can you help Baby Shark swim through the seaweed maze and get to the boat in the middle? The orange fish will guide you!

START

FINISH

Say goodbye to the Shark family.

doo doo doo doo doo doo!

Answers

Page 12

Page 36

Winner!

Page 24

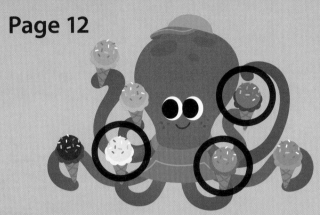

Pages 38-39

Baby Shark is in square: C10

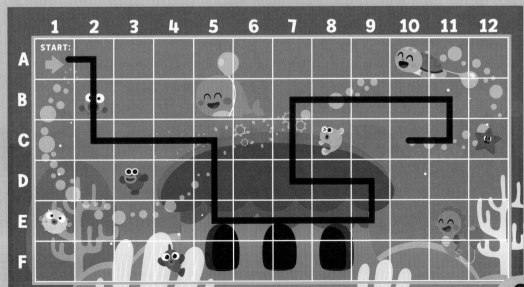

Page 42

Page 49

Baby Shark is in the picture 5 times!

Page 53

Page 54

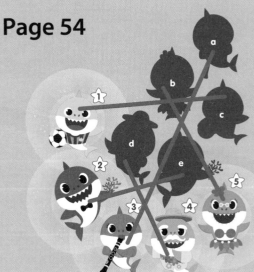

Page 61